OH! THOSE CRAZY DOGS!

A WINTER ADVENTURE

CAL

ILLUSTRATED BY
RACHAEL PLAQUET

BOOK EIGHT

To order additional copies of this book, contact:
Xlibris
844-714-8691
www.Xlibris.com
Orders@Xlibris.com

Illustrated by Rachael Plaquet

ISBN: Softcover   978-1-6698-3790-9
       EBook   978-1-6698-3789-3

Print information available on the last page

Rev. date: 07/18/2022

OH! THOSE CRAZY DOGS!

A Winter Adventure

Introduction

This is a story about 2 crazy dogs, their adventures and the mischief they get into.

They are very loving dogs, but they can't help getting into things.

Hi ! I'm Colby! I'm big and red and furry ! I love everyone but sometimes people are afraid of me because I am so big!

Hi! I'm Teddy Bear! I'm big and white and very furry! I'm not as big as Colby, but just about. Everyone thinks I'm cute and I put shows on for them.

He puts shows on for everyone, rolls on his back and kicks his legs up.

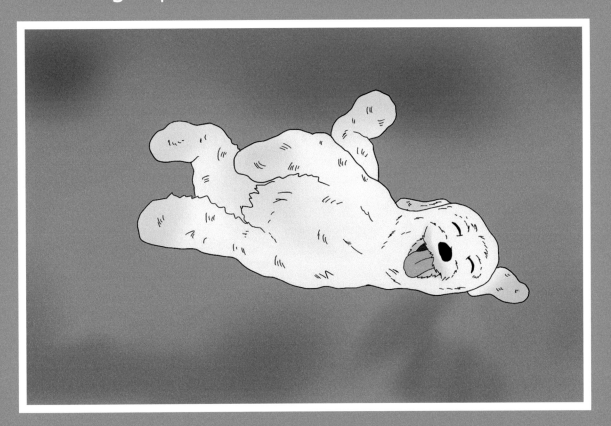

Our owners picked us out specially and brought us home to love and care for us. We love them too, very much. They give us everything and a warm loving home. We will call them Mom and Pop.

Sometimes we don't listen to them, especially me, Teddi Bear!

but our Mom and Pop love us anyway. Sometimes I get Colby in trouble. I can get him to do anything I want because he loves me too and can't say no. He protects me all the time.

A Winter Adventure

Colby And Teddi Bear were looking out of the patio doors. They were looking at the lake because they wanted to swim but mom said it was too cold. She said the lake was going to freeze over very soon. This was our last trip to the cottage until next spring. "Oh look!" exclaimed Teddi Bear, "it's snowing!" Colby said "and it's coming down really hard. We may not be leaving today."

"Let's go outside and play in it" said Teddi Bear. They both turned and looked at mom and barked to let her know they wanted outside. Mom looked at them and said "okay, but no lake!" Mom opened the patio door and Colby and Teddi Bear ran outside onto the porch and looked at the fresh snow piling up in the yard.

Colby looked at the lake longing to run into it, but remembered mom said no. "Let's go Colby !" said Teddi Bear. The 2 dogs ran down the steps into the snow. The ground was already covered with the new snow.

Colby and Teddi Bear started rolling in the snow with their legs kicking up in the air.

They lay on their tummies and stretched out, snuffling their noses under the snow and snorting when they came up above the snow. Oh how they loved the snow!

They both got up and Teddi Bear jumped up sideways, which Colby noticed and he knew what was coming next. Time for Teddi Bear to chase him.

Colby turned and ran. Both dogs ran quite differently. Colby ran with a large stride gallop, like a horse and Teddi Bear, well he ran low to the ground and his legs went so fast it was amazing. He could turn in a second.

Sometimes when Teddi Bear would turn to catch Colby, Colby would just jump over him and gallop away. It was very funny to watch.

Mom and pop would sit on the porch and laugh as they watched.

Colby and Teddi Bear were completely covered in snow because the snow stuck to their fur. It would actually build up until the dogs could barely move. They looked like snow dogs!

After awhile when they were tired, they lay down in the snow puffing and mom called them onto the porch. Mom and pop started taking all the snow off them.

Mom wrapped them in blankets and brought them into the cottage. "Wow" said Teddi Bear, "that was fun!" "Are you as tired as I am?" asked Colby. "yes I am" replied Teddi Bear. The two dogs fell asleep all wrapped up in warm blankets.

The next day the snow had stopped falling and mom and pop were finishing up the packing. A neighbor had ploughed the driveway out for them. We were going on the long ride again to go home.

There was snow everywhere as we started the trip home, but as we drove closer to home it got warmer and warmer and there wasn't any snow here!

We jumped out of the van and ran into the backyard expecting to jump into the pool. Mom and pop both laughed and said no, but we couldn't stop.

Argh, the water was cold, just like at the lake! Colby and Teddi Bear got out of the pool in a flash and shook off the water.

Mom came out with some blankets again to dry us off and warm blankets after. Mom said "I told you not to go in the pool. It's warmer here, but not warm enough to swim anymore."

Our supper was ready so we went into the house to eat and felt very content and tired. The next morning we woke up and mom and pop were outside doing something to the pool. We ran to the patio door and Teddi Bear said "Oh no, they're closing up the pool! They're putting the cover on it now!"

We watched as all the pool toys were put away. Now there was a solid blue cover on top of the pool.

Mom came to the patio doors and let us out. We ran to the pool but couldn't find it. "I know it's still here" said Teddi Bear "I can still smell the water" Teddi Bear slowly put his front foot on the cover. It moved a bit and he pulled his foot back quickly.

"What are we going to do now?" asked Teddi Bear. "We have to wait until winter is over now" replied Colby. "Snow will come here soon and after what feels like a long time, spring will come and they will open up the pool." "Ah heck" said Teddi Bear. "Let's play chase!" Colby started to run around the yard and Teddi Bear chased him. While Colby had an even gallop, Teddi Bear was very fast. He ran low and could take corners very fast.

Colby looked behind him and said "oh, oh I better do something or Teddi Bear is going to catch me!" Colby looked around and then ran right onto the pool cover and stopped in the middle.

Colby looked around. He was okay the cover didn't break or anything. It just went down a bit. It was bouncy like a trampoline. Hey, this was okay thought Colby. Teddi Bear screeched to a stop.

"Hey you can't go on there Colby" "looks like I can" said Colby with a smile on his face. "Come and get me!" Colby said. "That's not fair" yelled Teddi Bear. He tried to go on the cover too but he was afraid. Colby just sat there and laughed. "Ha, ha you can't get me!" Teddi Bear barked and sat down. "Well I guess you won this time Colby." Now what should we do?"

Suddenly pop was at the patio doors calling them in. "Let's go!" "It must be supper time!" said Teddi Bear and he ran to the doors with Colby right behind him. The next day Colby woke up and looked outside. "Teddi Bear it snowed outside! Look we can go play in it!

Oh mom and pop please let us out, let us out!" Teddi Bear gave a loud bark and mom heard him. She came over and opened the patio doors to the back yard. "Yay!" said Teddi Bear. "Let's go!" And away they went. Running through the snow, burying their heads in it, bums up in the air.

Both dogs were on their backs wriggling around with their legs up in the air. "Oh what a sight" said mom. These two dogs enjoy the snow just as much as the water!"

Teddi Bear started running after Colby and Colby jumped right over him.

Teddi Bear was running so fast he couldn't stop and ran right onto the pool cover. "Help" yelled Teddi Bear, "get me off this thing!" Teddi Bear was rolling and tumbling on the pool cover.

He suddenly realized it was like something he had seen before at a neighbor's house. "Hey this is just like a trampoline!" said Teddi Bear "come on Colby we have a trampoline over the pool now!" "Oh Teddi Bear, that's a safety cover for the pool. I don't think we're supposed to jump on that. Here, I'll help you off". "Aww are you sure we can't jump on it like a trampoline?" asked Teddi Bear. "Nope, sorry" replied Colby.

"Okay let's dig up a bunch of snow and make a great big pile. Then we can jump in it!" said Teddi Bear. Colby and Teddi Bear began digging the snow and it piled up higher and higher. Soon it was high enough to jump in.

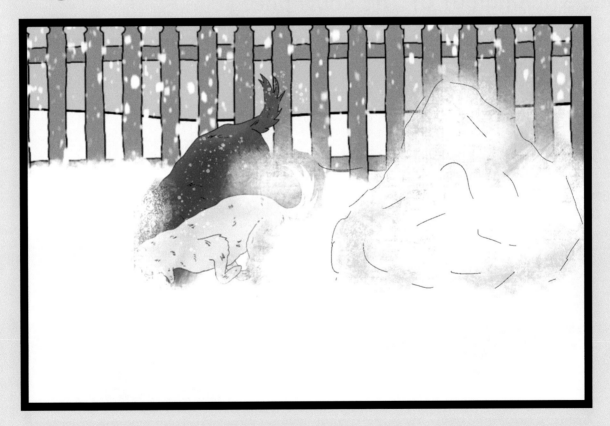

Colby and Teddi Bear looked at each other and Colby said "Ready, set, go!" they both ran toward the snow pile. Teddi Bear jumped right into the pile of snow and Colby went flying right over it! Pfluff. Only Teddi Bear's bum was sticking out of the snow pile.

Colby walked around the pile of snow and laughed and laughed. He heard some muffled words and watched as Teddi Bear's bum and legs wiggled.

Colby kept on laughing but he did pull Teddi Bear out of the snow. "That was so much fun!" exclaimed Teddi Bear while brushing snow from his face. "Let's do it again!"

So both dug at the snow until it was a big pile again. Then they both backed up to the edge of the pool. "Ready, set, go!" "Aargh" Colby had slipped and fallen backwards onto the pool cover. He did a couple of bounces and rollovers and stopped. This time it was Teddi Bear who was laughing at Colby. Ha, ha, ha, ha. Teddi Bear couldn't stop laughing at him.

Colby got up and very carefully stepped to the cement. Colby had a sheepish look on his face. "That was so funny" said Teddi Bear. "Come on, let's get ready to go again." said Colby. "Ready, set, go!" Both dogs took off as fast as they could go. And again Teddi Bear ended up in the middle of the snow pile but Colby ended up on the top of the snow pile.

It was soft snow so this time Teddi Bear stuck his head out on the other side with his legs sticking out behind him. Colby was still sitting on top with his legs dangling down on each side. Both dogs were laughing. "This is so much fun" yelled Teddi Bear. They were just covered in snow because it stuck to their hair. Both dogs had long hair too now because their mom and pop let it grow for the winter. They knew that the dogs loved to play in the snow and sit outside even when it was cold out.

Both dogs went jumping into the snow pile a couple more times until they were completely tired out. "Whew" said Colby "I think I need to rest a bit. I'm all tired out!" "Me too" said Teddi Bear. They both went to lie down on the patio in the sun. They warmed up quite quickly. Mom opened the patio doors and gave each of them a large dog cookie to eat. It was one of their favorite treats.

"Well what should we do now?" asked Teddi Bear. "I wish we could see Digger and Tyse again" replied Colby. "I miss them" Colby sat up and walked over to the fence. He put his front paws up on the fence and looked over it. "No, I don't see Digger anywhere. I wonder where he lives. It must be close enough because he found us." Teddi Bear, who was sitting by the gate in the fence looked up and said, "look it's snowing again!"

Colby was walking toward Teddi Bear when suddenly the gate opened. Pop walked through the gate carrying some parcels. Before he had a chance to close the gate, Teddi Bear ran out.

Pop dropped his parcels and yelled at Teddi Bear. "You come back here! Teddi Bear come back!" Pop had forgotten to close the gate because he was so surprised at Teddi Bear running out. And guess what? Colby took a chance and ran out the gate too! Pop tried to grab him but Colby was too fast! "Colby and Teddi Bear come back here now!" pop yelled. But they were gone running as fast as they could.

"Let's try to find Digger now!" said Colby. "Oh boy are we going to be in trouble when we get back" said Colby sadly "but I really want to find Digger. I'm worried about him." "Really? Why?" asked Teddi Bear. "I don't know" replied Colby. "It's just a feeling I have. The way he said something about going home one time. The way he said it bothered me and I keep thinking about it." "Okay let's go search for him." said Teddi Bear. And off they went walking up and down the sidewalks calling Digger.

They found Digger laying under a large shrub in someone's yard. "Digger! We were worried about you! Where have you been? Is this your home?" Colby was so excited he was nearly bouncing. "No" said Digger "I was just trying to keep warm. I don't have long thick hair like you guys do. I only have short thin fur that doesn't grow."

"Well can't you go into your home?" asked Colby, nodding toward the house. "That isn't my home" said Digger. "Well, where is your home then?" asked Colby. Digger just looked at them sadly. "I don't have one anymore. I go where ever I can get warm and there is always food in garbage bags." "What? Oh Digger why" exclaimed Teddi Bear. "My family moved and left me here a couple of years ago." said Digger. "I found you guys for friends and that makes me happy. We have fun together. "Oh Digger, I'm so sorry" said Colby near tears.

"Come back to our place. Maybe you can stay for awhile. It might take a bit before our mom and pop realize you don't have anywhere to go but come on, let's try." Colby, Teddi Bear and Digger started walking back home.

Teddi Bear saw a big snow bank where someone had shoveled their driveway. "Woo let's jump" he said. All of them ran for the snowbank. "mmff" said Teddi Bear as he ended up buried in the middle, legs hanging out. "aargh" said Digger who ended up below Teddi Bear. "Yay! I win" said Colby who was sitting on top. "I'm the king of the castle!

Ha Ha! Teddi Bear and Digger laughed. They all got down, shook the snow off and continued on home. When they got home the three dogs just stood on the front porch and gave a bark.

Immediately the front door opened. Colby said "Come on Digger´ All three dogs ran in. Mom said "You are naughty dogs for running away! Where did you go?

Hey who is this? Come on out you go. Go home." Digger started to walk toward the open door when Colby and Teddi Bear surrounded him and wouldn't let him go. "Well, I guess you don't want him to leave. Okay he can stay for awhile."

The dogs went into the kitchen where there were 2 bowls of food. Colby ate some and left some for Digger. Teddi Bear ate some and left some for Digger. Mom couldn't believe her eyes. The dogs were sharing their food with their friend! Mom put another bowl on the floor and put food in all three bowls.

After they ate, Colby said he was tired and needed a nap. They all went into the living room. Colby jumped on the couch, Teddi Bear looked at his bed and told Digger he could sleep in it. It was soft and warm and very comfortable. "Thank you Teddi Bear" said Digger. Teddi Bear lay down on the floor beside Digger and put his head on the pillow of his bed. They all went to sleep.

Mom and pop walked into the living room and saw the three dogs sleeping together and again they couldn't get over how they had shared. Mom and pop looked at each other and said

OH! THOSE CRAZY DOGS!

Thank you for choosing this book to read. Please watch for book 9 coming out soon!

Books in the Oh! Those Crazy Dogs!
Series written by author CAL

Printed in the United States
by Baker & Taylor Publisher Services